Dragon Farts

Fire in the Hole!

J.B. O'Neil

Table of Contents

FREE BONUS: "Dragon Farts" Audiobook

Hey gang...if you'd like to listen to the hilarious audiobook version of Fart Ball while you follow along with this ebook, you can download it for free for a limited time by typing this link into your browser:

http://funnyfarts.net/dragon-farts

Enjoy!

Grounded

Saturday is the most perfect day that the human race ever invented. You can go to the movies, play video games all day, play baseball until you break your bat, or build the most incredible snow fort your neighborhood has ever seen. Whatever the season, whatever the weather, wherever you live, you can always count on Saturday to be awesome. Even if you're one of those kids that likes school, you can do homework on Saturday. It's perfect for everybody!

As you can see, I have a lot to say about Saturday. So you can imagine that I felt pretty lousy when one Saturday, I was grounded.

Why was I grounded? For trying to win the science fair. I really tried hard to make a working replica of the human digestive system. I spent HOURS on it, and I was hoping to get first place! But no matter what I said, the teacher said it was "inappropriate," and my parents thought the same thing.

I learned something that day: as long as you're a kid, you can never model a pooping butt and have people take it seriously. The kids will laugh, but the adults will yell at you.

As I sat on my bed, I wished that I could be somewhere where everything gross I did was considered absolutely fart-tastic. A place where everyone thought I was super cool.

And that's when the wizard of sickly supremacy, Hurlin, showed up.

The Wizard Hurlin

A sparkling blue mist drifted in through the open window of my room. It started to swirl and spin all about, until it made a miniature cyclone. Lightning crackled, thunder roared, I wet my pants, and then a figure emerged from the center of the cyclone.

He was a tall old man, with a sharp nose, sparkling eyes, a majestic flowing beard, and shimmering blue robes. He wore a pointed hat decorated with stars and moons. His face was set with a dignified frown, like a great and wise teacher who has just come into the classroom.

This incredible, powerful man took a step

forward out of the storm that he created, looked me square in the eye, and opened his mouth.

Then he screamed "*HRGLF*" and puked all over the floor.

"Ew, what the heck man?" I said.

He wiped his mouth with his beard, gasping for breath and sweating. "My apologies," he said shakily, "my sincerest apologies, master Milo. I am the Great Wizard Hurlin, of the land of Smellsalot, and our world is in great danger. You are the only one in all the universes who can help us! There's no time to lose!"

I jumped off the bed, being careful to walk around the puddle of vomit that was soaking into the carpet.

"Slow down there, Mr. Abracadabra. How do you know my name?" I asked.

To Another World!

"I scried it in my crystal ball," Hurlin said. "It told me that a young knight would come from a faraway world, and use the powers of farts, boogers, and burps to save the kingdom."

"Wow! Your crystal ball has good taste, Hurlin," I said.

"The Princess of Smellsalot has been kidnapped by the evil Dragon of Arm's Pit, and she will soon be devoured," Hurlin continued. "She is the only heir to the throne. If she dies, then Smellsalot will be thrown into chaos and destroyed. You, Milo Snotrocket, must become a

Knight of the Round Buttcheeks, and go on a quest to slay the dragon and save the princess!"

"I'm sorry, what kind of knight again?" I said.

"Of the Round Buttcheeks," Hurlin repeated.

I grinned and slapped Hurlin on the back, which was a bad idea because it made him gag and nearly puke again. "You got yourself a hero, Hurlin! I got nothing better to do anyway. When do we leave?"

"In just a minute," Hurlin said. He puts his hands on his knees and started breathing heavily. "I just feel a little bit...sick...just give me a moment."

"But there's no time to lose, didn't you just say that a little bit ago?"

"Yes, yes I did but... I'm... I'm a little unsteady on my feet...time travel is magically intensive, don't you know."

It ended up taking about twenty minutes for Hurlin to settle his stomach with some crackers and Tums, but then finally, we were off in his magic cyclone to the land of Smellsalot!

The Castle of Smellsalot

One second I was in my room and the next I was outside a giant medieval castle. Its banners were flying high in the wind, the sun shone down on its mighty moat, and all around us was a deep, dark forest. It was the perfect Medieval scene like in every comic book, TV show, and movie that you've ever seen.

Except for Hurlin, who bent over and heaved up a pathetic little dribble of spit and stomach juices onto the ground. He coughed, wretched, coughed again, and then finally stood up.

"Welcome, *hrk*, to Smellsalot," Hurlin gasped.

After a few minutes Hurlin felt good enough to walk to the drawn-up drawbridge.

"Guards! Guards of Smellsalot! It is I, the court wizard Hurlin! Open, in the name of the princess Burpetta!" Hurlin commanded. He managed to sound powerful and wizardish for the first time since I'd seen him.

For a little while there was no reply. Then a guard poked his head over the wall and looked down at us.

"No!" the guard said sulkily.

"No?" Hurlin replied, "What the devil do you mean, no?"

"You swept out of the castle this morning without so much as a 'goodbye Steve, see you later,' and that wasn't the worst part. You didn't wish me a happy birthday!" the guard said.

Hurlin groaned and shuffled his feet. "I was in a hurry to save the kingdom! This is no time to be childish!"

"There's no excuse for rudeness," Steve said. He sniffled.

"Oh for the love of-...Steve, I'm sorry. Happy birthday. I'll get you a unicorn, to make up for it."

"You promise?" Steve said.

"Yes, I promise!" Hurlin said impatiently, "now let down the blasted drawbridge!"

The drawbridge came down, and Hurlin and I crossed it.

"Are there real unicorns in Smellsalot, Hurlin?" I asked.

"Of course not, don't be silly. I'm going to have to paint a perfectly good donkey white and stick the fat end of a carrot up its nose," Hurlin grumbled.

A Knight's Challenge

We had just gotten to the castle courtyard when a knight on horseback wearing full plate armor suddenly burst from the keep.

"Halt! Halt, ye knave," the knight said. "You trespass upon the mighty Castle of Smellsalot! None shall enter without proving their worth!"

Hurlin sighed and rolled his eyes. "Is this really necessary, sir knight?"

"Aye," the knight said.

"You know that this is the prophesied one that I left to collect only about an hour ago, yes?" Hurlin said.

"Aye. That doesn't matter! What if he's a coward?"

"Oh fine then! Have it your way, you muscle-bound oaf," Hurlin grumbled.

I looked up at the knight. "How do I prove my worth?" I asked.

"Ye must defeat me in a joust, on the field of honor!"

"Will someone teach me how? I've never done that before," I said.

"Aye!" the knight replied. "Hasten to the field to be fitted, and as the sun sets, we shall duel!"

The knight turned his horse and prepared to gallop away.

"Wait! If we're going to fight we should know each-other's names, right? I'm Milo," I said.

"You are a courteous foe, I will grant you that," the knight said. "I am called Sir Poopsalot!"

"Poopsalot?" I said.

"Aye, Poopsalot!" Sir Poopsalot said, and then he left.

The Field of Honor

The Field of Honor was behind the castle keep. Hurlin took me to a tent, where a bunch of hustling and bustling skinny guys measured me with string and poked me with needles. Finally, they got together the smallest set of platemail they had, and an openfaced helmet that almost wasn't too big for me.

Then they lifted me into the saddle of a giant black horse, and gave me a long steel lance. They kept trying to make me hold it in one hand, but the thing weighed about twenty pounds. The only thing I could do was hold it in both hands and balance it on top of the horse's head, which the horse didn't like one bit.

"Hey, I still don't know what to do," I said to one of the irritated skinny guys as they walked me and the horse onto the field.

"It's simple," the man said sharply. "You just go as fast as you can, and try to smash your lance into Sir Poopsalot and knock him off his horse."

"That sounds kinda dangerous," I said.

"Oh, not so much. Only four or five knights die a season," he said. Then he smacked my horse on the butt and said "go get him!"

All of a sudden, my horse was galloping full-speed down the field, and charging up the field was Sir Poopsalot!

I was so scared, I panic farted. Luckily, at the same time, my horse farted, and the combined blast shot me forward. As soon as my lance hit it was jolted out of my hands, but Poopsalot was so surprised, he fell right off his horse.

Milo, Knight of the Round Buttcheeks

I had no idea how to stop the horse, so all I could do was sort of flop off its back once it had slowed down enough. Before I could struggle to stand, Sir Poopsalot lifted me up onto my feet.

"Truthfully, I never thought that you would best me," he said, "but today you have proven your worth and courage to me. Welcome, Sir Milo, to the Knights of the Round Buttcheeks!"

Sir Poopsalot walked with me into the castle keep, where a group of seven knights stood waiting in full armor.

17

"Sir Milo," Sir Poopsalot said, "allow me to introduce to you the Knights of the Round Buttcheeks:

"Sir Buttavere the Wise, who together with me leads the order;

"Sir Burpsival the Brave, our mightiest warrior;

"Sir Urine of the John, who has served with us longer than any other knight;

"Sir Gasisbad, who often consults with the wizard Hurlin about magical and mystical secrets;

"Sir Borsusall, who keeps our spirits high with his songs and stories;

And Sir Bob."

"What does Sir Bob do?" I asked.

"Now Sir Milo," Sir Poopsalot said, "join us, for a feast in your honor! It shall be a most worthy occasion!"

"Sounds great, I'm starving!" I said. "But what about Sir Bob?"

"Gather together, good knights!" Sir Burpsival

cried. "Let us waste no time, or mead, in celebrating Sir Milo's strength! I would hear of how he unseated Sir Poopsalot."

"With a mighty wind!" Sir Gasisbad said, "just as Hurlin foretold!"

And, together, the Knight of the Round Buttcheeks entered the Great Hall.

The Feast

Counting me, there were now nine knights of the Round Buttcheek. We each took a seat at a round table in the main hall, which I noticed was painted to look like a pair of cheeks mooning the ceiling.

The feast was amazing, particularly because they didn't serve a single vegetable. We ate breads, cakes, candies, and berries, and lots and lots of meat. I think just about every animal in the area was represented by at least one dish, and my favorite one, the Meat Surprise, definitely had all of them.

I ate two helpings of everything, but the knights

made me look like I was on a diet. They devoured everything on the table, washing it all down with gallons of mead, ale, and cider. Not a single person drank water that night; I stuck to fruit juice.

When it was all finished I sat back, patted my swollen gut, and then let out a table-shaking burp.

I was about to cover my mouth and say, "excuse me," but the knights all laughed and clapped.

"Someone's praising the cook!" Sir Urine yelled. "I second those kind words!" Then he let out a burp even louder than mine.

Soon, we were all burping as loudly as we could, trying to see if anyone could belch hard enough to break one of the wooden mugs or shatter the stained glass windows. No one did, but it was a lot of fun.

"Well, Sir Milo, I think it is time for bed," Sir Poopsalot said, wiping a tear from his eye. "We're up with the sun tomorrow. It's time to save the Princess!"

"HUZZAH!" cried the other knights. "Yeah, huzzah!" I added.

We Ride

"Up with the sun" was actually an understatement: when I was shaken awake from the pile of straw I'd had to sleep in it was still dark outside.

The other knights and I groggily ate a breakfast of cold meat and fruit. I'd secretly hoped for cereal, but they didn't have Lucky Charms in medieval times. When we were done, Sir Poopsalot ordered us to go out to the stables and inspect the horses.

When we got there, the stable boys has just finished spooning out the horse's breakfasts. I figured that the stable would smell like farm animals and poo, but this stable smelled even worse than that. It brought tears to my eyes.

"Ugh! What do you feed these horses, Sir Poopsalot?" I said. I had my nose pinched shut so I sounded weird and tinny.

"The horses of Smellsalot are fed a diet that ensures quick, safe travel over any field or hill," Sir Poopsalot said proudly. "Nothing but the finest cabbage and beans!"

This definitely explained how my horse's fart from the other day had rocketed me forward; normally, only my own farts are strong enough to do something like that. I was liking the land of Smellsalot more and more.

After the horses finished eating we saddled them up and got ready to leave. We sat on our horses outside the castle of Smellsalot while the wizard Hurlin gave us directions to Arm's Pit, the dragon's lair.

Then, we set off, fart-riding away into the rising sun. The quest had begun!

The Green Knight

After a while, when we'd reached an open field, a knight wearing all green approached us.

"I am the Green Knight," The Green Knight said, "and this is my Field of Honor. Any who wish to pass must defeat my challenge!"

"And what is that, good sir knight?" Sir Poopsalot asked.

"Whosoever can get their snotty spit the farthest from this line, that I shall draw in the ground with my sword, shall win the challenge. If any of you best me, then you are free to continue. But if not, you must turn back!"

"I'll accept that challenge," I said. This knight was a knight of boogers, but when it comes to boogers, I'm the king.

"We accept as well," Sir Poopsalot said.

The Green Knight drew his line on the ground, and then hawked up and spat a giant loogie, as big as a golf ball. It flew up into the air, and then splatted down almost fifty yards away.

It was immediately obvious that we were in trouble. Not even I can spit that far, even when the wind is at my back. One by one the other knights did their best, but no one came even close.

Then it was my turn: I was our last hope. I figured I could get 30, maybe 40 yards, but I'd still be way short. Then I realized something.

"Sir Green Knight: you just said "get your spit the farthest, right?"

"That's so," the Green Knight said gruffly.

I hawked up a big loogie, then walked past the line. The other knights watched me, open-mouthed with amazement, as I walked past all the other boogers, up to the big snot ball, and then spat a few feet past it.

"You never said we couldn't cross the line," I said. "We win."

The Might Excalibur

The Green Knight was so impressed with my cleverness that he let us go on. We made camp for the night, then by the afternoon of the next day, we passed by a beautiful sword, stuck deeply in a large boulder.

The other knights began to ooh, ahh, and point at it. "What is it?" I asked.

"It must be the legendary Sword in the Stone...the mighty Excalibur!" Sir Poopsalot cried. "Tell us the legend, Sir Borsusuall!"

"They say that whosoever pulls out the Sword in the Stone, shall someday become the rightful King of the Land," Sir Borsusall said. "A thousand knights have tried the sword, but none have ever succeeded."

"Well, today I shall make my mark, and start my legend," said Sir Burpsival. "Stand aside!"

Sir Burpsival jumped off his horse and walked up to the sword, spitting into his palms and rubbing them together.

"For Smellsalot!" he cried. Then he gripped the handle with both hands, bent his knees, and pulled with all his might.

And the sword popped right out like someone had greased it, making him fall back on his butt.

The other knights exploded into angry shouts of disbelief. "I am he! I am the rightful King of Smellsalot!" Sir Burpsival said. "If you would try me, then dare take the sword yourself! I shall replace it, and it will await my hand, and my hand alone!"

"I will try!" said Sir Urine. Sir Burpsival put the sword back, and everyone held their breath to see what would happen.

Sir Urine gripped the sword, braced himself, and desperately pulled up on the sword. It popped free like a cork from a bottle.

The Pitiful Excalipoor

Once Sir Urine pulled out the sword, every knight gave it a try, and every knight pulled the sword easily from the stone. Even Sir Buttavere, who was kind of a nerd.

"What is this witchcraft?" Sir Gasisbad said. "Are we all worthy, then, to rule Smellsalot? Are we to go to war?"

"I think I just loosened it up too much," Sir Burpsival said. "I was the first to draw the sword. I am the only one worthy to rule!"

The knights started to fight and argue. During their quarrel, I inspected the sword in the stone.

It was definitely a beautiful blade, so I could see why the other knights had gotten distracted. But because of that, they'd missed something important: there was a poem carved into the rock, just above the slot where the sword rested.

"Hey, everyone! Listen to this," I said:

"Who takes Excalipoor, from its fit
Must surely be, a great idiot!
For this sickly sword, this wimpy blade,
Has always losers, from winners made."

"Ye Gods! We've made a terrible mistake!" Sir Borsusall said. "This is not Excalibur: this must be the cursed Excalipoor!"

"The Sword of Cowards? The Humbler of Heroes? The Meekstone of the Mighty?" Sir Buttavere said.

"None other. Whosoever wields Excalipoor shall never taste victory, no matter how weak and pitiful the enemy. We had better leave it alone," Sir Borsusall said.

And so we left Excalipoor, shining in its stone sheath, for some other unlucky person to find.

Thrun's Contest

We had nearly made it to Arm's Pit when we were stopped at the edge of a deep wood by our greatest challenge yet: a giant, three-headed, incredibly stinky, troll named Thrun.

"We have a simple test for trespassers," Thrun said to us. "Each of you may ask us a single question. If we cannot answer it, then you may pass. But if we answer them all, then you shall all be cooked on a spit and eaten. Agreed?"

"Agreed!" the knights said. Then we put our nine heads together to think of the toughest, most mind-boggling questions we could.

But it was no use. Thrun's three heads worked together in a way our nine couldn't: Thrun was ugly, and Thrun was big, but Thrun was a genius too. If I brought him on Jeopardy, he'd definitely win.

But I hadn't asked my question yet, and as I walked up to Thrun, I thought of only one that could possibly help us out.

"Which head is the smartest head, Thrun?" I asked.

"Well, everyone knows that the left brain is devoted to reason and logic, so that would of course be me," said the left head.

"But everyone knows that the right brain is the seat of creativity and abstraction, so it's really me," said the right head.

"As the bridge between both, I obviously have all the strengths of both sides," said the middle head.

"Or none of them," said the left.

"Is that an insult?" said the middle.

"If you're so smart, you figure it out," said the right.

And all of a sudden, Thrun was arguing with himself. Then, he was screaming at himself. Soon, he was throwing punches at all of his heads, until finally, he knocked all his own brains out. We hurried past him before he came to.

Arm's Pit

Finally, after days of travel and lots of danger, we had made it to the mouth of Arm's Pit. It was a dank, dark cave, and in that cave lived a dragon.

"Well guys, here we are," I said. "I've never slain a dragon before, but over these last few days, I feel like we've really gotten close to each other. We have each other's backs, and I know that with your help, we can do this! Let's go!"

I expected a loud "huzzah" and a bunch of drawn swords, but the reaction I actually got was mostly kicking at dirt and awkward coughing.

"Sir Milo, over these last few days, you have shown incredible bravery, cunning, resourcefulness, and wisdom. It's clear that there is no other knight more deserving, or more capable, of the honor of slaying the dragon," said Sir Buttavere. "In fact, you're surely the greatest knight we have ever quested with. We think that we would be only hold you back. Go and rescue the princess, and we shall wait for your triumphant return!"

"But, but I-" I stuttered, but the other knights all pushed me toward the cave, saying "you're the prophesied one!" and "you'll do great, go Sir Milo!"

I had a feeling that all of those compliments and encouragements were for some other reason, but after a while, I did feel pretty good. So I agreed to go into Arm's Pit, by myself, without any idea how to kill the dragon or save the princess at all.

What could go wrong?

The Dragon's Den

I swallowed my fear and stepped into Arm's Pit.

I walked through darkness for a long time.
Warm, smelly darkness. Just what you'd expect
from a place called Arm's Pit.

Then I saw a faint light ahead of me, and I
jogged toward it as fast as I could, given how
hard it was to breathe in there. When I reached
the light, what I saw took what was left of my
breath away.

It was an enormous cavern, and it was
absolutely stuffed with treasure. Gold coins,
silver cups, shining jewels from every color of

the rainbow, suits of armor and gleaming weapons...this place had everything. Even a dragon.

That's right, the dragon was there. He was impossible to ignore, because he was nearly as large as the treasure trove he slept on. As the reptilian monster breathed, tiny jets of flame shot from its smoking nostrils. It was a classic dragon.

And, in a nearby iron cage, there was also a classic princess.

"Pst! Squire! Are you here to rescue me?" the princess whispered.

"Yeah, but I'm not a squire," I whispered back. "I'm Sir Milo, of the Round Buttcheeks!"

"Fantastic! Oh, I knew Sir Poopsalot would send someone," she whispered. "Quickly, come unlock the cage, the key is laying just out of my reach. But, be as quiet as you can: the dragon has very good-"

Just then I accidentally let out a big, juicy fart.

"-hearing."

The Dragon Awakens

Instantly, the dragon jumped to its four feet. I had no idea that a creature so huge could move so quickly, and it scared another squeaky fart out of me.

"Not even mice are foolish enough to break into my home, though a mouse is what I hear," the dragon bellowed. "Yet before me, I see a human! So, are you a man or a mouse? I would say neither, as you appear to be just a boy. Speak! Why are you here?"

I was trembling all over, and I'd broken into a cold sweat despite the heat in the room. But I didn't let my voice shake like my body did when

41

I replied.

"I'm Sir Milo Snotrocket, Knight of the Round Buttcheeks. I'm here to rescue the princess, who you kidnapped, in the name of Smellsalot!"

The dragon laughed, unkindly. "You? A pathetic little ant like who hasn't even gotten his first pimple? Ridiculous. You will not be rescuing the princess: you'll be lucky, if you can rescue yourself!"

Then the dragon turned around, and let out a giant fiery dragon fart! I raised up my shield to protect myself, and the shield melted before the heat. I threw it aside and then drew my sword. I charged at the dragon, hoping I could slice at its feet and surprise it into falling.

But when I swung my sword, it shattered on its skin.

So now I had no shield, no sword, and an angry dragon. So here's what I did:

I ran.

You'd do the same thing!

"I'll burn it! I'll burn all of Smellsalot for this, coward!" The dragon roared, and it chased me with fire.

One Last Plan

I escaped from Arm's Pit just ahead of a blast of firey fart that nearly burnt me to a crisp. The other knights looked frightened, but not surprised.

"I knew it, not even Sir Milo could defeat the dragon," Sir Buttavere groaned. "No knight, no matter how strong or stinky, can hope to slay him. We can't win!"

"We need a plan," I said. "You guys weren't much help, I gotta say. So help me out now. There's got to be a way for us to beat the dragon!"

"It may be hopeless, but you're right Sir Milo: we have not been much help to you at all," Sir Poopsalot said. "Think, good knights, think: for all of Smellsalot!"

So we all hunkered down on the ground, and we thought, and we pondered, and we brainstormed. We drew diagrams. We argued a lot. Finally, after many hours of hard work, we had nothing.

I was thinking that Sir Buttavere had been right: we really couldn't win. That's when I had the only good idea we'd had.

"Good knights, it's true: there's no way we can win," I said. "But, is there a way that the dragon can lose?"

"What do you mean?" Sir Burpsival said.

I explained my idea as quickly as I could.

"Ye Gods, Sir Milo, you may have done it again!" Sir Poopsalot cried. "Quickly, good knights, make haste! We haven't a minute to lose!"

Together, we charged on our horses back the way we'd come. Then, less than a day later, we came back, for one last try.

The Peace Offering

Once again, I headed into Arm's Pit, this time with the cheers and hurrahs of my fellow knights pushing me on. I came to the treasure room, and the dragon was sitting on his haunches.

"And here I was, expecting a parade of knights to come trying to vanquish me. But all I get is the same man-mouse from before. And with a new sword to boot! Going to try to give me a splinter again, man-mouse?"

I drew the new sword from its sheath, and I heard the dragon catch its fiery breath. The sword shone in the golden firelight, a polished piece of brilliance.

"I was wrong to try to sneak into your home, dragon," I said, dropping to one knee and holding the sword out with both hands. "As a token of my apology, I'd like to offer you this beautiful sword, in exchange for sparing Smellsalot. Please don't destroy it because of what I did."

The dragon paused for a minute, weighing the decision. Then, with two of its giant claws, it picked up the sword.

"I will take this sword," it said, "and I will spare no one! You think that you can bargain with me?"

"Oh no! You're...you're a monster!" I cried.

"I'm a dragon, fool! Thanks for the toothpick, I'll use it to get the shreds of you out from between my teeth!"

Fartscalibur!

The dragon lunged and snapped with its terrible teeth. It mighty jaws closed around my armor, and for a second I was sure I was about to be bitten in half.

Then I heard a loud crack, and the dragon whimpered in pain. The dragon's teeth had broken!

It raised up a claw to stomp me, but suddenly it yelped and fell over from a cramp. Next it tried another dragon fart, but only a wimpy little pooter came out with a few tiny sparks. It swung its tail at me, but hit it on the wall and bruised it.

"What...what is this? What's happening to me!?" the dragon roared.

"I can explain, dragon: you just took the Lamest Blade, Excalipoor! It makes the strong weak, and the weak ridiculously lame! Now meet my other sword, and this one's going to finish you: Fartscalibur!"

I held my hands under my butt and farted out an enormous sword made of the stinkiest, bravest gas I could make. Then I waved it under the dragon's nostrils.

"Ugh! Oh, it's so stinky...and I'm so weak...I can't stand it! I'm done with this place!" The dragon said. Then he slithered out of the cave as fast as he could, and was never seen again.

I ran over to the princess' cage and unlocked it with the key. Then, together, we went outside to join the other Knights of the Round Buttcheeks. Victory for Smellsalot!

The Princess' Reward

We had a party in the wilderness that night,
then we all rode home to Smellsalot. When we
got there, Hurlin was waiting outside the castle
for us.

"Well done, Sir Milo!" He said. "The princess is
saved, the knights have returned home safely,
and the prophecy has been fulfilled. But now, it's
time to return home."

I looked back at the assembled Knights of the
Round Buttcheeks, and felt sad that I'd have to
leave.

"You guys all thought I was super cool, just for

being who I am. I'll never forget you."

Sir Poopsalot nodded, then drew his sword. "Three cheers for Sir Milo!" he cried, and the other knights joined him. It was a great going-away present.

Then the princess stepped towards me.

"Sir Milo, you succeeded where any other knight would have failed. If not for your bravery, and your stinky farts, my kingdom would be in ruins. Courage, and manliness, like yours deserves a very special reward."

"Like what?" I asked.

"Close your eyes, you handsome young man," she replied.

I immediately felt sick to my stomach. I was sure of it: she was going to kiss me. This is why I don't get girls! This was going to be super gross, and not in the good way!

Please don't kiss me please don't kiss me please don't kiss me...

Then, a light, stinky burp washed over my face.

I opened my eyes just in time to see the princess doubled up laughing, before everything turned into swirling blue mist.

Happily Ever After

And suddenly, I was back in my puke-smelling room. The chunks of vomit were starting to dry into the carpet now, and the sun was setting. It was almost dinner time. I'd spent over a week in Smellsalot, but here it'd only been a few hours!

It was going to be a huge pain to try to clean the upchuck from Hurlin, but I didn't really mind. I'd finally gotten the praise and respect due to me as an awesome person and master farter. No matter how old I got, or how famous, I knew that I would never forget my time spent with the Knights of the Round Buttcheeks.

And, I gotta admit: for the first time in my life, I felt like I might have fallen in love...

More Books by J.B. O'Neil

Hi Gang! I hope you liked "Dragon Farts." Here are some more funny, cool books I've written that I think you'll like too...

http://jjsnip.com/fart-book

And...

http://jjsnip.com/booger-fart-books

Silent but Deadly...As a Ninja Should Be!

http://jjsnip.com/ninja-farts-book

Did you know cavemen farted?

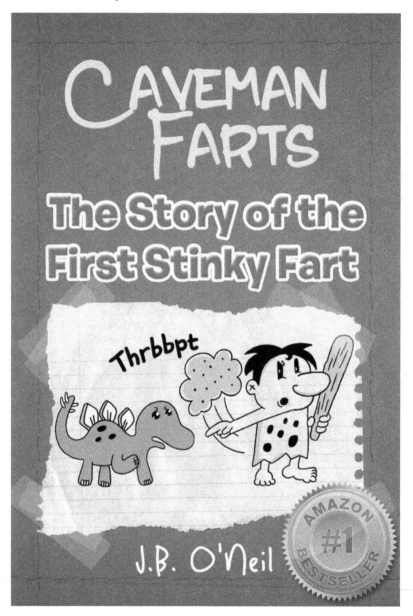

http://jjsnip.com/caveman-farts

Think twice before you blame the dog!

http://jjsnip.com/dog-farts

A long time ago, in a galaxy fart, fart away...

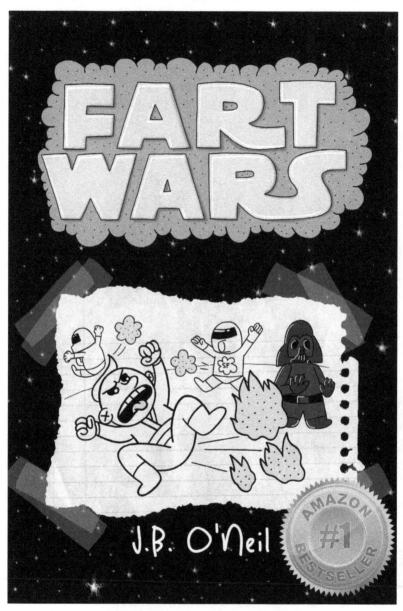

http://jjsnip.com/fart-wars

It's a turd, it's a sewer, no! It's...

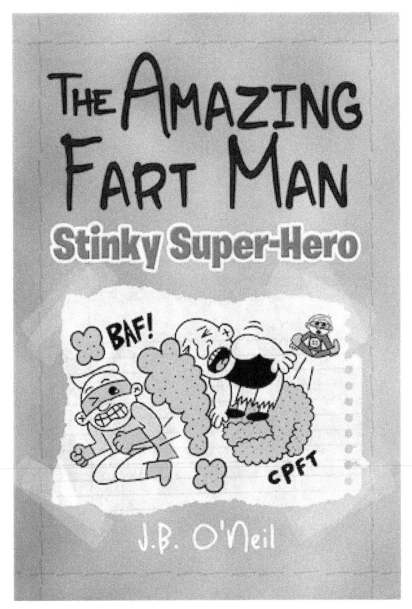

http://jjsnip.com/fartman

We Are the Farts! The Mighty Fighting Farts!

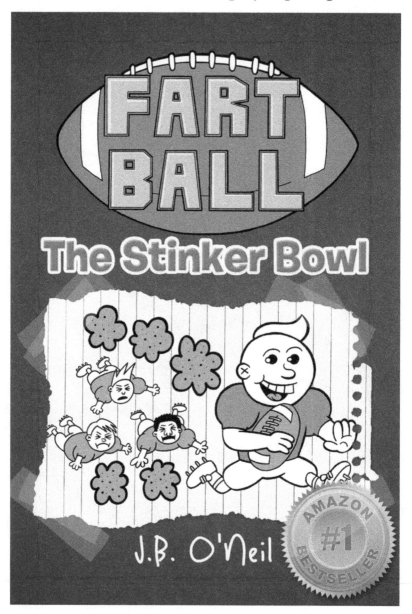

http://jjsnip.com/fart-ball

Farts can be Spooky, too:

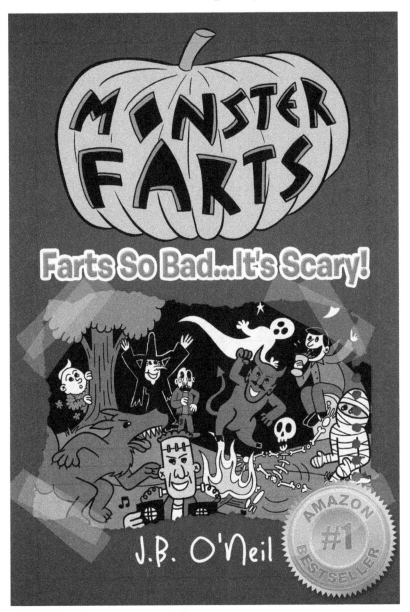

http://jjsnip.com/monster-farts

CPSIA information can be obtained
at www.ICGtesting.com
Printed in the USA
LVHW031720110320
649741LV00003B/592

9 781495 298301